WAITING-FOR-PAPA
S T O R I E S

BY BETHANY ROBERTS

ILLUSTRATED BY SARAH STAPLER

H A R P E R & R O W , P U B L I S H E R S

Waiting-for-Papa Stories
Text copyright © 1990 by Barbara Beverage
Illustrations copyright © 1990 by Sarah A. Stapler

Library of Congress Cataloging-in-Publication Data
Roberts, Bethany.
  Waiting-for-papa stories / Bethany Roberts ; illustrated by Sarah
Stapler.
    p.   cm.
  Summary: As Papa Rabbit's family anxiously awaits his return home,
Mama Rabbit eases their fears by telling funny stories about Papa.
  ISBN 0-06-025050-X : $. — ISBN 0-06-025051-8 (lib. bdg.) :
$
  [1. Rabbits—Fiction.   2. Fathers—Fiction.   3. Humorous stories.]
I. Stapler, Sarah, ill.   II. Title.   89-36589
PZ7.R5396Wah   1990   CIP
[E]—dc20   AC

To my wonderful, loving husband, Bob—
who, like Papa Rabbit, always makes it home

The Rabbit family peeked anxiously out the window of their cozy home. Papa Rabbit had gone out early that morning, and hadn't yet returned. Visions of owls and weasels and hunters with guns entered the heads of his family.

"I know what we need," said Mama Rabbit. Eight pairs of round little eyes looked at her.

"We need some Waiting-for-Papa stories," said Mama. She gave one last stir to the carrot stew, gathered her children around her, and told these tales.

RABBIT DINNER

Once a papa rabbit was late coming home for dinner.

"I'm going to *be* a dinner if I don't find my way out of these woods soon," he said.

Just then an owl hooted. "Who-o-o are you?"

"I'm an owl," said Papa.

"You look like my dinner," said the owl.

"Nonsense," said Papa. "I have feathers." He wiggled his ears. "And wings," he said, flapping his arms. "And I can fly!" he exclaimed, as he bounded into the bushes.

"That's funny," said the owl. "I could have sworn that was a rabbit."

Once again Papa started for home. Soon he saw a hunter.

"What's this?" said the hunter.

"I'm a rock," said Papa.

"You look like my dinner," said the hunter.

"Nonsense," said Papa. "I'm round. And I'm brown," he said. "And I can roll away!" And he rolled away into the bushes.

"That's funny," said the hunter. "I could have sworn that was a rabbit."

Once again Papa started for home. But he saw a weasel.

"Ho, *ho*! Dinner!" said the weasel.

"Nonsense," said Papa. "I'm the rain." Huge tears ran down his cheeks. "And I'm thunder," he said, thumping his hind feet. "And I'm lightning!" he shouted, running lickety-split out of the woods.

"That's funny," said the weasel. "I could have sworn that was a rabbit."

Papa started for home, as fast as he could go. "A papa rabbit never misses dinner!" he said.

PAPA'S GARDEN

Once a papa rabbit loved flowers. He decided to plant a garden. One day a flower popped up.

"Hello, Flower," said Papa. "What can I do for you?"

"I'm a flower, and I need rain," said the flower.

So Papa got a bucket of water and sprinkled the flower with rain.

"Is that better, Flower?" asked Papa.

"I'm a flower, and I need sunshine," said the flower.

So Papa moved the flower from the shade into the sunshine.

"Is that better, Flower?" asked Papa.

"I'm a flower, and I need fresh breezes," said the flower.

So Papa got a fan, and fanned fresh breezes on the flower.

"Is that better, Flower?" asked Papa.

"I'm a flower, and I have nothing to do," said the flower.

So Papa planted the flower in his hat. He put the hat on top of his head. Then he and the flower went for a walk. Together they saw frogs in the pond, birds nesting in trees, and a ladybug in the grass.

"Is that better, Flower?" asked Papa.

"Yes," said the flower, "that's much better, thank you."

A WALK IN THE RAIN

Once a papa rabbit went for a walk in the rain. "Nothing like a walk in the rain," he said.

Other rabbits passed him by, with their umbrellas and galoshes.

"That rabbit doesn't even know enough to get in out of the rain," they said. "Tsk, tsk." And they went into their houses, slamming their doors behind them.

"What's wrong with rain?" said Papa.

It rained very hard. Soon there were puddles all over the ground.

"Oh, good," said Papa's feet, as he splashed in the puddles. "We were dirty anyway."

It rained harder. The puddles turned into a pond.

"Oh, good," said Papa's knees, as he waded in the pond. "We were dirty anyway."

It rained even harder. The pond became a lake.

"Oh, good," said Papa's ears, as he swam in the lake. "We were dirty anyway."

At last the sun came out. It dried up all the water.

"What a fine walk I've had," said Papa. "And I am clean all over."

The other rabbits saw the sun and came back out of their houses.

"My," they said, as Papa walked past, "what a clean rabbit!"

PAPA AND THE KITE

Once a papa rabbit was flying a kite. The kite flew higher and higher, until she was as high as the clouds.

"Come back, Kite," said Papa. "It's time to go home."

"No," said the kite.

"It's getting late," said Papa.

"No," said the kite.

"You must be tired," said Papa.

"No," said the kite.

"Listen," said Papa, "I know you're having fun up there. But we can come back tomorrow."

"No, no, no," said the kite.

"Oh, my," said Papa. "I feel very sleepy." Papa yawned loudly.

"M-m-m," said the kite. She yawned a little, too.

"My feet are tired, my eyes are tired, my bones are tired," said Papa. "Sleepy, sleepy."

"Sleepy, sleepy," said the kite. She closed one eye.

"Soft clouds, soft pillow, soft bed," said Papa.

"Soft," sighed the kite. She closed the other eye.

Papa pulled the kite down to the ground. He carried her home.

"We'll fly another day," said Papa.

"M-m-m," said the kite. "Another day."

PAPA GOES FISHING

Once a papa rabbit went fishing. He rowed out
to the middle of a lake. A breeze came along and
blew off his hat.

Papa watched his hat sink into the water.
"Well, that is that," he said.

Papa got ready to fish. He baited his hook. He
threw out the line.

Soon he felt a tug. Papa pulled and pulled.

"I've got one, I've got one!" cried Papa. He
pulled in ... an old shoe.

"Well," said Papa, "it's not a fish. But a shoe is nice."

Papa baited his hook again. He threw out the line. Soon he felt a tug. He pulled and pulled.

"I've got one, I've got one!" shouted Papa. He pulled in . . . an old bottle.

"Well," said Papa, "it's not a fish. But a bottle is nice."

Papa baited his hook again. He threw out the line. Again he felt a tug. He pulled and pulled.

"I've got one, I've got one!" yelled Papa. He pulled in . . . an old tire.

"Well," said Papa, "it's not a fish. But a tire is nice."

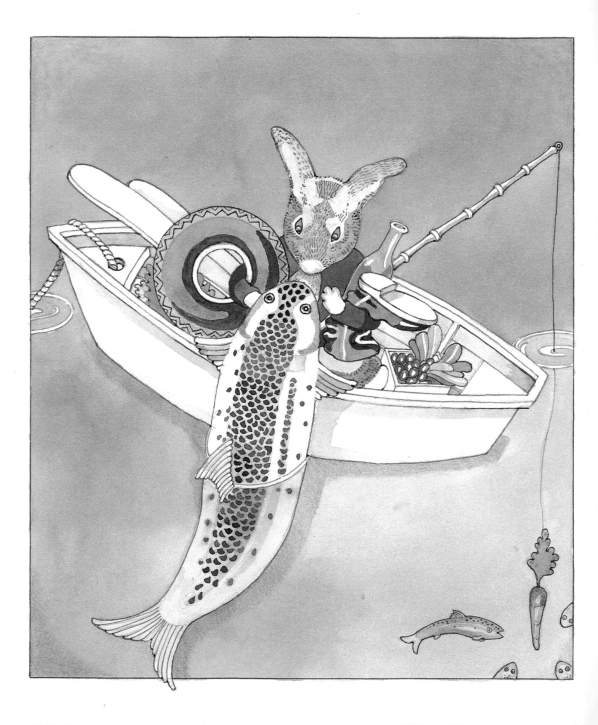

Just then an old fish swam by. He saw Papa with the shoe, the bottle, and the tire.

"Hey," said the fish, "give those back. Those are mine!"

So Papa threw back the old shoe. He threw back the old bottle and the old tire.

"Thank you," said the fish. "And now I have something for you."

The fish dove into the water. He swam back with Papa's hat. Papa put his hat on his head.

"Even a wet hat," said Papa, "is very nice. And that is that."

PAPA'S EAR

One morning a papa rabbit looked at himself in the mirror. His left ear wouldn't stand up straight.

"Up, up!" said Papa.

"Rise and shine!" said Papa.

"Last one up's a rotten egg!" said Papa.

But his ear just flopped.

"I know what we need," said Papa, "—a good, hearty breakfast."

Papa had a plateful of eggs, hash browns, orange juice, toast, and three blueberry muffins. But his ear still flopped.

"Push-ups!" said Papa.

"A nice cold shower!" said Papa.

"Deep breathing!" said Papa.

But hard as Papa tried, his ear just wouldn't stand up straight.

"Hm-m," said Papa. "I think we need a nice, brisk walk."

So Papa took his ear for a walk.

"Hear the birds sing!" said Papa.

"Listen to the crickets chirp!" said Papa.

"Hear the wind blowing through the trees," said Papa.

But nothing seemed to help.

At last they came to the vegetable garden. Papa kneeled down. He put his ear to the ground.

"Listen to the sound of carrots growing!" said Papa.

At that, Papa's ear perked right up. It stood straight and tall.

"The sound of carrots growing is music to my ears," said Papa.

"Nothing sweeter," sighed his ear.

PAPA'S SKIS

Once a papa rabbit got a pair of skis. That afternoon he decided to go skiing.

"Great idea," said the left ski.

"Great idea," said the right ski.

And off they went. Papa skied and skied.

Soon they came to the top of a hill.

"Which way do I go?" wondered Papa.

"To the left!" said the left ski.

"To the right!" said the right ski.

The left ski went left. The right ski went right. And Papa fell—*plunk!*—right on his nose.

Papa got up to try again.

"Which way should I go?" wondered Papa.

"To the right!" said the left ski.

"To the left!" said the right ski.

The left ski went right. The right ski went left.
And Papa fell—*plunk!*—right on his nose.

Papa got up to try again.

"Which way should I go?" sighed Papa.

"To the left!" said the left ski.

"To the right!" said the right ski.

"Hold it!" said Papa's nose.

The nose sniffed the air. A whiff of carrot cookies was in the breeze.

"Straight ahead!" said the nose.

The left ski went straight. The right ski went straight. And Papa skied down the hill straight to his rabbit home.

"We thought you'd gotten lost in all that snow," said Mama Rabbit.

"Lost? Not me," said Papa.

Papa munched a carrot cookie. "The nose knows," he said.

"Look, Papa's home!" cried Mama.

Eight little rabbits tumbled out the door to meet him.

"Papa! We thought you'd been shot by a hunter!" said one little rabbit child.

"Or caught by an owl!" said another.

"Or by a weasel!" said a third.

"Nonsense!" laughed Papa. "A papa rabbit never misses dinner!"

He kissed his wife on the tip of her nose and hugged each member of his family more than once. Then he sat down to dinner—and it wasn't even cold.